Summer of Shame

The sequel to
An Alien Spring

by
Anne Schraff

Perfection Learning Corporation
Logan, Iowa 51546

Cover Illustration: Mark Bischel
Cover Design: Deborah Lea Bell

1 MARK SCOTT AND his friend Hugh Velliers watched the dusty black MG sports car crawl down the main street. The car rolled to a stop in front of the *Marnard Tribune* office. Out stepped a young woman in flame-red slacks, red sweater, and black pumps. She carried a designer briefcase.

Mark's eyes widened. You didn't often see strangers in Marnard, let alone strangers this beautiful.

"Man," Hugh gasped, "she looks like a fashion model or something."

The boys watched as the woman disappeared inside the *Tribune* office. They sipped on their ice-cold sodas in Mark's pickup, eager for the woman to reappear.

School had been out for just a few weeks and already the two were bored. It had been an incredible spring—so incredible that everything else paled by comparison.

Early in the year, violent tornadoes had set people on edge. Then one night in March, a mysterious fire started in the Velliers' cornfield. Most of the field had burned, leaving only a large depression in the earth.

Not long after that, a teenager named Edward Thomas showed up in school. He and his brother, Jules, were big, powerful guys. At first they'd seemed to be deaf and mute. And their strange behavior caused some folks in town to believe the brothers were aliens from outer space.

Then a lot of people in town got sick. Near panic resulted when it was rumored that the brothers were spreading a virus. The panic climaxed when an angry posse had gone after the brothers and the sheriff's daughter was almost killed.

"Hey, look," Mark said, spotting a flash of red. "She's coming out. And she's looking at *us*, Hugh."

"Smile, Mark," Hugh laughed. "This might be our lucky day. Could be she's a talent scout for one of those teen magazines. Maybe she's looking for some handsome country boys to photograph."

Mark laughed too. "Yeah, right."

The boys held their breath as the young woman strolled over to the truck. "Hi, guys," she said. "My name is Kyla Raines. I'm a social worker, and I was wondering if you could help me."

Mark and Hugh exchanged puzzled looks. *A social worker?*

"There were two boys here some weeks ago named Edward and Jules Thomas. Did you know them?" Ms. Raines asked.

"Yeah, Edward was in my class," Mark replied. "He and his brother lived at the old Marvin place."

"Everybody figured they were aliens or something," Hugh put in. "One of them ripped the heads off our chickens and almost choked me. He was like an animal."

Ms. Raines' deep blue eyes widened. "Is that right?"

"Yeah," Hugh said. "And two guys from around here, Larry and Bill, they got in a fight with Edward. They even tried to tie him to a tree. Well, Edward yanked the ropes off like they were pieces of thread. Then he flattened them both."

"It was in self-defense," Mark pointed out.

"I see," Ms. Raines said. "They told me in the newspaper office that a posse was organized to find the boys. A man named Steve Scott spirited them away—"

"That's my dad," Mark interrupted

proudly. "The posse was really getting wild. Guys were shooting at anything that moved. They even shot the sheriff's daughter by accident. Dad might've saved the Thomas boys from a lynching. The sheriff was so impressed that he hired Dad to do deputy work for him."

Ms. Raines seemed delighted to have found Mr. Scott's son. "Well, then, you're the one I want to talk to. I'm very anxious to find the Thomas boys."

"Why is it so important?" Mark asked.

"Well, obviously they're living alone, fending for themselves. Hungry, uncared for. We can't let that happen, can we? There are wonderful foster homes for boys like that where they'll be warm and well fed." Ms. Raines' scarlet lips parted over dazzling white teeth in a beautiful smile.

"Uh, by the way, I'm Mark Scott and this is Hugh Velliers," Mark said. "You want to follow me home and talk to my dad?"

"Oh, that'd be wonderful," she said. She hurried to her MG.

In the pickup truck Hugh remarked, "She sure seems like a strange social worker."

"Yeah," Mark agreed. "I mean, there's lots of runaway kids. Why is she so interested in those guys?"

As Mark pulled into the drive, he spotted Mr. Scott painting the porch. He came down the steps and waved to his son. Then turning to Ms. Raines, he nodded and said, "Hello, there. What can I do for you?"

"Hello, Mr. Scott. I'm Kyla Raines," the young woman said as she stepped out of her car. "Your son and his friend were kind enough to ask me out here to speak with you. I'm a social worker. The county asked me to locate the Thomas boys, see if they need help, and give them as normal a life as possible."

"I see," Mr. Scott said. He slowly wiped blue paint off his hands with an old rag.

"We realize the boys aren't normal," Ms. Raines continued. "Who knows what kind of misery they're living in?"

Mark's father winced at the words "not normal." After his nervous breakdown, he'd been described as "not normal" too. For months he'd gone without work because people were afraid to hire a mental patient. Everybody'd treated him differently, as though he weren't quite human anymore.

"I understand you snatched the boys from under the noses of a bloodthirsty posse," Ms. Raines said. "So perhaps you know where they are now?"

"Well, I wouldn't call Sheriff Poulsen and his men bloodthirsty," Mark's father said, rubbing his chin. "Running scared is what they were. Folks were blaming those poor kids for everything that went wrong around here. Everything from the three-day flu to holes in a cornfield."

"Could you take me to the place where you hid them, Mr. Scott?" Ms. Raines asked. She was beginning to sound impatient. Mark wondered if she was from a large city. People from large cities always seemed in a hurry.

"I suppose I could," Mr. Scott said. "But you won't find them there. It's over near Springville. They got out of the cabin fast and headed into the woods. I've been back there a couple times, and it's always been deserted."

"Still, I'd appreciate it if you'd show me where they were last seen," Ms. Raines said.

"Well, now, I don't mean to be telling you your business, ma'am," Steve Scott began. "And I've got a lot of respect for social workers who look out for the welfare of kids. But I don't think these boys could be pushed into foster care at their ages. They'd be too skittish for that."

Ms. Raines smiled. "I know you mean well, Mr. Scott. But, you see, we've got to do what we can. If they're underage, they can't be allowed to live in the woods like wild things."

"Well, I'll drive you over there, Ms. Raines. It's a rough road. I don't know that your little sports car could handle it," Mark's father said.

Ms. Raines quickly climbed in the pickup cab beside Mr. Scott. Mark and Hugh jumped in the back, and the truck took off.

"There's something fishy going on, Hugh," Mark said as they flew down the road, the wind whipping their hair. "Social workers haven't got time to track kids like this."

"What do you think she's up to?" Hugh asked.

"Maybe there's been trouble in some

neighboring town," Mark suggested. "Maybe they heard about what happened in Marnard. And now they figure the Thomas boys have come *their* way."

"Who is *she* then?" Hugh wondered. "A private investigator? She's sure gorgeous, whoever she is."

They bounced down the rutted road Mr. Scott had taken the night he'd saved the Thomas boys from the posse. When they arrived at the run-down cabin, Mr. Scott parked nearby.

As the group walked to the small building, Mark's father said, "Well, here it is, Ms. Raines. It was just a lean-to to begin with. And the wild storms we've had certainly haven't helped matters."

Ms. Raines walked around the cabin, stooping and examining the ground. "Hmmm, what's this?" she asked.

Mark stooped beside her. "What?" he asked.

"This looks like slime," she said. "Black slime...gobs of it..." She sniffed the matter. "Ugh...what a stink!" Her eyes glistened with excitement.

Mr. Scott came over. "You looking for

footprints? The rains washed them out long ago," he said.

"Foul-smelling black slime," Ms. Raines said. She wrote something in a notebook she'd slipped out of her purse.

Ms. Raines straightened up and looked at the white pine and cedar trees. "Lots of broken branches."

"Yeah, we had some bad tornadoes this year," Mark said.

"What makes the grass look crushed like this?" Ms. Raines asked. She shoved her toe into the trampled grass.

"Any number of things," Mr. Scott said, his eyes narrowing. He was getting impatient. He had a porch to paint before dark. Mark knew his dad couldn't finish it tomorrow since he'd be busy in the helicopter. Sheriff Poulsen wanted him to scout the countryside for some missing cars. There'd been a rash of auto thefts lately.

"Now then," Ms. Raines said, "I've heard that both boys had unusually large hands."

"Yeah. Big, apelike hands," Hugh agreed. "When I felt those hands around my throat, I thought I was a goner."

Ms. Raines came closer. "Apelike?" she repeated.

"Yeah. That Jules, he reminded me of a big, wild ape," Hugh said. He was enjoying the young woman's rapt attention.

"Come on, Hugh," Mark snapped. "Jules just happened to be a big guy. Lots of big people around." Honestly, Mark thought, will it never end?

"Well," Ms. Raines said, "I've taken up too much of your time already. You've all been very kind. If you'll just drive me back to my car now, I won't trouble you anymore."

As the group walked to the pickup, Mark's father asked, "Ms. Raines, excuse me for being kinda confused. But what do black slime and bent grass have to do with finding those boys the county is so worried about?"

Ms. Raines hesitated a moment. Then she said, "Anything that can give me a clue about the boys and their where-abouts is important."

"What does slime tell you?" Mark whispered to Hugh.

Hugh shook his head.

Back at the Scott house, Mark's father hurried back to his painting job, but Ms. Raines lingered. She wanted to talk to Hugh a bit more. Not that Hugh seemed to mind. Any lady who looked like her was worth his time.

"You know, Ms. Raines," Hugh said, "the first time I saw you I figured maybe you were a new teacher at Marnard High. Man, was I glad. Most of our teachers are really *old.*"

Ms. Raines smiled. "That's sweet, Hugh. You know, what you said about Jules' hands interested me. How wide across would you estimate them to be?"

"Big! Maybe twice a normal guy's hands," Hugh said.

"Nah, not that big," Mark scoffed. "Just a regular big guy's hands."

"They were around *my* throat, man," Hugh said. "And they were huge!"

Ms. Raines' eyes took on an almost manic excitement. Mark wondered again just who the woman was. He sincerely doubted she was a social worker as she claimed. Whoever she was, Mark had a sinking feeling that she boded no good for the Thomas brothers.

2 MS. RAINES CONTINUED plying Hugh with questions. "Their height—what would you think? Down at the *Tribune* I was getting all kinds of guesses, from well over six-feet-five to seven feet or more."

"Maybe Jules was seven feet tall," Hugh said.

"Nah," Mark said.

"At least six-feet-six," Hugh insisted.

"Very big creatures then," Ms. Raines said.

"Creatures?" Mark repeated. "Did you say *creatures?* That's what the social welfare department is calling lost kids these days—'creatures'?"

Ms. Raines' almost constant smile faded. She gave Mark a sharp look. "I didn't mean it the way it sounded, Mark."

"Well, it kinda bothered me. Last spring when everybody was going crazy around here, people were calling those poor guys 'alien creatures.' I was just afraid maybe you thought they were aliens too," Mark said.

Ms. Raines laughed. "Not at all. I don't believe in all that UFO stuff. Science has proven to us that there's no intelligent life in near space. If there *are* intelligent beings in space at all, I'm sure they wouldn't land in Marnard." She finished with a smug snicker. It was as if she thought of Marnard as a backwater town, unfit even for aliens from outer space.

Mark was slowly growing to dislike Ms. Raines. But at the same time, he could tell Hugh was developing a major crush on her.

The next words out of Hugh's mouth confirmed Mark's suspicions. "I'm almost eighteen," Hugh pointed out to Ms. Raines. "I bet you aren't more than twenty-two or something."

"About right," Ms. Raines said, a little smile playing around her lips.

"All right," Hugh said with a grin. "I'll bet you even like a lot of the same stuff that I do."

Mark felt embarrassed for Hugh. What a klutz! Hugh was flirting with Kyla Raines. As if a woman like her would be interested in a farm boy from Marnard— or *any* boy for that matter! She'd find Hugh no more interesting than Mark would a little ten-year-old girl with sticky bubble gum all over her face.

"Don't be a jerk, man," Mark said softly as Ms. Raines went to her MG to search for something. "You're just a punk kid to her!"

"You're just jealous, man," Hugh said. "Now you know how I felt last spring. Remember when Jeannie Bryant gave me the cold shoulder and fell all over you? Well, now the shoe's on the other foot."

Last spring, a student named Jeannie Bryant had returned to town after being gone for several years. Every guy at Marnard High had angled for dates with her—especially Hugh. When Jeannie ignored every guy but Mark, Hugh had been crushed.

"She's a *woman*, Hugh!" Mark said. "You've been calling her 'Ms. Raines,' for heaven's sake. Don't go making a fool of yourself!"

"Pea green," Hugh taunted. "Pea green with envy!"

Kyla Raines returned from her car with a camera. "Hugh, may I take a photo of you?"

Hugh glanced at Mark and grinned. "Sure thing," he said to Ms. Raines.

"You're a doll," she said, clicking away.

"I want to keep track of the people I've talked to about the Thomas boys. It's for my files."

"Look," Hugh said eagerly, "there's lots more I could tell you about those guys. Why don't you come over to my house for dinner tonight? Grandpa could tell you stuff too."

"That's so sweet of you, Hugh. I'd love that," Ms. Raines said. "I'm a real sucker for down-home cooking!"

"Great. We live about a quarter mile from here—you can see our place from here. See the big silo?"

"I see it," Ms. Raines said. "And I'll be there."

"Around seven. That's when we eat. Mom's a real good cook."

"You're such a sweetheart," Ms. Raines said. She waved and climbed into the MG.

Mark and Hugh watched the car until it left the driveway.

"You see? *You see?*" Hugh gloated. "She called me a 'doll' and a 'sweetheart'! She goes for me, man! Maybe that grinds you, but it's true!"

Mark Scott stared at Hugh. They'd been

friends and neighbors since they were both toddlers. Hugh was a good kid—a slim guy with soft blue eyes and slightly oversized teeth. It wasn't surprising that girls were attracted to him—high school girls, that is. But Kyla Raines?

"Man, I bet she's thirty years old if she's a day," Mark said.

"No way she's thirty years old! She's twenty-one or something," Hugh said. "She's gorgeous!"

"Lots of those pretty actresses are in their thirties," Mark pointed out. "You can't tell. Kyla Raines is probably old enough to be your mother!"

"Man, you're so jealous, you're going nuts!" Hugh cried. "Don't you wish she was coming to *your* house tonight instead of mine? Don't you wish she was wanting to sit on the porch swing under the big fat moon with *you* instead of me?"

"Hugh, you know what your grandpa would say if he heard you? 'You been in the sun too long, boy, and you're tetched in the head!' " Mark laughed, but Hugh only snorted and stalked off towards the Velliers farm.

Mark shrugged and went to join his dad on the porch. He stooped down and grabbed a paintbrush.

"It's about time, son," Mr. Scott said with a smile. Then he asked, "What do you make of that Raines woman, Mark?"

"Same thing I'd make out of a seven-dollar bill, Dad," Mark replied.

"Not for real, eh? Same here. To tell the truth, I'm a bit scared. I'm afraid she means no good for those Thomas boys." Mark's father sounded worried.

"I got that same feeling. Dad, what do you figure happened to those guys, anyway?" Mark asked.

"Probably they're in the woods, living off the land, sticking close to the river. It can be done. Long as you don't get out on the prairie, there's always a tree to hide behind. And plenty of fish to be taken; berries too. Then they'd likely be borrowing stuff from orchards—enough to survive. I wouldn't begrudge them that," Mr. Scott said.

"*Who* are they, I wonder," Mark said.

"I'd guess they came from a family with a troubled history. Parents died and left the boys to make it on their own as best they can. Seems like they'd had little contact with people. I wish all that nonsense hadn't happened this spring. Then Edward might have done real well in school and Jules might've lost some of his fears.

"If only folks had shown them a little tolerance when they were out at the Marvin place," Mark's father went on. "Little by little the boys would have come out of their shells. But it wasn't to be. Ignorance and prejudice saw to that, son." Mr. Scott shook his head sadly. Mark knew his dad was reliving his own sad experiences too. It wasn't very long ago when the shadow of mental illness had made Mr. Scott an outcast in his own community.

Mark's mother looked out onto the porch from inside the house. "Looking good, guys," she said.

Grace, Mark's younger sister, peeked out too. "Who was the lady in the MG?" she asked.

"She claims to be a social worker trying to find the Thomas boys and put them in a foster home," Mark said. "But it sounds phony to me."

Grace would be a sophomore next year. She was a tall girl, a real power on the girls' basketball team. "Maybe the Thomas boys are her own long-lost children," Grace said. In addition to her athletic skills, Grace had a vivid imagination.

"Yeah, I got it!" Mark's sister went on. "She gave them up for adoption when they were babies. Now she's gone on to great success as...um...yeah, a world-famous fashion designer. And um...she read about these weird kids in the *Marnard Tribune*. Bingo, she remembers her past and how she gave up those adorable babies for adoption. She sees they've been mistreated and mistaken for aliens and now she wants to rescue them."

"Yeah, right," Mark laughed. "Ms. Cover Girl is the mother of two hulking guys."

"Wait," Grace commanded. "See, she fell in love with a rugged mountain man— a diamond in the rough. I can see him now: a big, furry guy with blue-black hair and turquoise eyes. But theirs was a star-crossed love, and she had to give up the kids because...ummm..."

"A grizzly bear ate Dad," Mark said,

continuing the farfetched story. "And she put the two little boys in a canoe and sent it down the river. And those guys just had to fend for themselves all these years. Though maybe they had the help of a friendly raccoon and a skunk called Stinko. How's that? How am I doing?"

Grace giggled. "Oh stop it, *you*. You think you know it all. Well, I just hope those Thomas boys have a nice, cozy place to stay wherever they are. And I hope their neighbors are nicer to them than people were around here."

"Amen to that," Mark's mother said heartily. "It just makes me sick to think how those boys were treated. Abused by Bill and Larry, chased by a posse with bloodhounds. I wouldn't want to see an animal treated that way, let alone two boys!"

For the rest of the day, the Thomas boys were on Mark's mind. So was Kyla Raines. Mark hoped that the woman wasn't in town to cause any trouble. He also hoped that Hugh wasn't in for a broken heart.

The next morning Hugh came over to shoot baskets with Mark. Hugh remained silent about the previous night. Finally, Mark couldn't stand it any longer.

"Well, Hugh," he asked, "you going steady now with Kyla Raines?"

"How'd you like a fat lip?" Hugh snapped.

"Uh-oh. Trouble in paradise," Mark teased, sending a ball through the hoop. "Well, you know how these May-December romances are."

"All she wanted to do was talk about those Thomas boys," Hugh complained, missing an easy shot. "She couldn't get enough of it. She wanted the gory stuff, like the headless chickens. I sorta exaggerated, just to make her happy. I told her the Thomas boys ripped the heads off of sheep too, not just chickens. And boy did she go for *that!*"

Mark stopped in his tracks. A flash of anger charged through him. But deeper than the anger was a chill blast of fear. It was starting again. The rumors and the ridiculous superstitions.

Mark just prayed the Thomas boys had run far enough this time.

3 HUGH GLARED AT his friend. "Well, I happen to know there *was* a headless sheep found in a ravine at that time," he said defensively. "Who's to say *they* didn't do it?"

"A pack of wild dogs did it, stupid!" Mark yelled furiously.

"Well, don't make a federal case out of it," snapped Hugh. "Besides, what harm can someone like Kyla Raines do to the Thomas boys anyway?"

Mark didn't have an answer to that. He'd give just about anything to know who that nosy woman was. And why all the interest in the gory, sensational details?

A few days later, Kyla Raines appeared at the Marnard Mall, carrying her notebook. She interviewed every teenager who'd ever walked past Edward Thomas in the halls of Marnard High. Mark hovered nearby. He was determined to get a line on just what she was trying to do.

Ms. Raines hit pay dirt when Bill Bryant and his friend Larry Dunne came along. They were more than happy to talk to the beautiful stranger.

"Yeah, me and Larry can tell you plenty about Ed Thomas," Bill said. "I got the scars to show from meeting up with him. Now, I'm a pretty strong guy when it comes to dealing with ordinary people. But this guy was something else."

Larry quickly chimed in. "He came at us like a madman. I'm telling you, he tried to kill us. That Ed Thomas isn't human. *He's an animal!*"

Mark entered the conversation. "It's a good story—but it's only about half the story. Why don't you tell Ms. Raines how you got mad at Ed and tied him to a tree and tried to whip him. How he finally got loose and gave you a taste of your own medicine."

"No way," Bill said. "It didn't happen like that."

"You admitted it to Sheriff Poulsen," Mark said.

"Your father and Sheriff Poulsen forced us to say that, just to clear that ape Ed Thomas," Bill protested. "Your dad was really excited, Mark. We were scared of him 'cause he's crazy too. So we told him what he wanted to hear."

Mark's blood began to boil. Leave it to Bill Bryant to bring up that stuff about Mark's dad having a nervous breakdown. "You're a liar!" Mark yelled.

"Calm down, Mark," Ms. Raines said. "I didn't want to start a fight. I'm just trying to collect information that will help me find the Thomas boys."

"I don't know what you're doing, Ms. Raines," Mark snapped. "But I don't think you're trying to *help* anybody but yourself!"

Ms. Raines smiled in a condescending way. Then she turned back to Bill and Larry and urged them to finish their tale.

"Edward came at us with this whip," Larry said. "He was slashing at us. We tried to fight him off. He busted my ribs with his fist—those hands of his were like stone. He broke my arm like it was a matchstick!"

Ms. Raines was writing quickly now, her pen flying across the notepad.

Bill joined in. "I lost a couple of teeth and my whole jaw was almost smashed. I felt like I'd been hit by a truck. I never saw somebody so strong and so wild. And all the time, he was laughing and grinning.

When I saw that big red mouth of his, know what I thought of?"

"No—what?" Ms. Raines asked.

"A gorilla. One of those big monster apes, with saliva dripping all over," Bill said with satisfaction. "I'm telling you—if that thing ever comes around here again, I'm gonna be ready. And not with fists this time."

At that moment, Jeannie Bryant, Bill's cousin, came out of the jeans store, carrying a bulging sack. For a short time during the spring she and Mark had hung out together. Then Jeannie had joined Bill in a cruel prank directed against Edward Thomas. Fortunately, Mark had caught on just in time to what Bill and Jeannie were doing. So the prank backfired. Since then, Mark and Jeannie had hardly spoken to each other.

"Here's my cousin Jeannie," Bill said to Ms. Raines. "She can tell you what a brute Edward Thomas is."

Jeannie glanced towards Mark. She'd never forgiven him for dropping her. While she'd dropped plenty of boys herself, she'd never had one brush her off.

Jeannie knew how the whole Scott family had stood up for the Thomas boys. Now she sneered at Mark. "Oh yeah," she said. "That Ed Thomas tried to attack me one day after school. I tried to scream, but he put one of those huge hands over my mouth. Who knows what would have happened if some people hadn't come along then!"

"That's a filthy lie, Jeannie, and you know it," Mark said. He knew she was lying about Edward Thomas only to get back at him.

"Mind your own business, Mark," she said. "Everybody knows why your family defended those freaks. It was because your dad was weird too."

Jeannie turned her attention back to Ms. Raines. "Everybody at school wondered why they let that Edward come to classes. He was a menace. He couldn't talk—just grunted like some kind of animal. And he had these scary eyes. They gleamed just like a wolf's." Jeannie shuddered. "Everybody was terrified of him."

"Ask Tanya Bailey," Mark said to Ms. Raines. "Ask Monica Gilsner. They'll tell you Ed was a nice guy who didn't bother anybody. Ask *them* if you want the truth, Ms. Raines. But maybe you don't."

Ms. Raines closed her notebook and smiled coldly at Mark. "Thanks for the suggestions, Mark. Well, I've got to get going." She strode out of the mall without looking back.

The rest of the day was uneventful. That evening, the Scotts sat out on their freshly painted front porch drinking lemonade and enjoying the cool breeze from the river.

"Find any of those stolen cars, Dad?" Mark asked.

"Matter of fact, I spotted a suspicious area in Rinkers Grove," Mr. Scott said with a satisfied grin. "Sheriff Poulsen went over there and solved six cases of stolen cars in one fell swoop. Nabbed a pair of hotshots running the operation. They were cutting up the cars for parts."

A shout from the driveway interrupted the conversation. It was old Mr. Velliers, waving a newspaper in the air.

"Didja see this, Steve?" he shouted.

"I hope another flying saucer didn't

land near here," Mr. Scott chuckled.

"We're famous," Sam Velliers shouted. "My grandson's picture is right here in a big coast-to-coast newspaper."

"What are you talking about?" Mark grabbed the paper. He noticed it was a tabloid. The glaring black headline jumped out at him:

"Bigfoot and Abominable Snowman Join Forces to Terrorize Peaceful Marnard!"

The subheadline screamed,

"Hairy Monsters Leave Trail of Death, Destruction in Prairie Town!"

"I can't believe I'm reading this," Mark gasped. "She's a tabloid hack, Dad! Kyla Raines lied about being a social worker just so she could write this garbage!"

"It's not garbage," Mr. Velliers insisted. "My grandson told the truth. One of them creatures almost choked the life out of him."

Mark's father read the article out loud:

A pair of murderous monsters have stalked this once-quiet prairie town, attacking citizens and mangling animals. Handsome Hugh Velliers, a local high school senior, told of being nearly strangled by one of the creatures. The creature almost killed two other boys, William Bryant and Larry Dunne, pounding them into unconsciousness. A third attack on a young woman was thwarted by the intervention of passersby.

"Oh man," Mark groaned. "How could she do this?"

Mr. Scott continued:

The attacks on animals have been even more bloody. One monster beheaded a flock of chickens in a mad midnight frenzy. The marauders also left behind headless sheep after another rampage.

This would not be the first time such half-human, half-ape creatures have terrorized people. In 1948 in

Nepal, a Norwegian prospector was attacked and mauled by one of the creatures called Yetis in that part of the world. Also in Nepal, in the 1950s, Yetis battered five people to death.

Nor is this the first time these creatures have struck in the United States. On June 25, 1973, a couple was frightened by weird shrieks in the woods near Murphysboro, Alabama. Peering through the darkness, they glimpsed an eight-foot-tall creature smelling strongly of foul river slime. The couple barely escaped with their lives. The creature left in his wake a trail of crushed grass, broken trees and black slime.

This reporter personally observed similar telltale signs at the spot the creatures dubbed "the Thomas boys" were last seen. All too plain was the devastating work of the creatures who have wreaked havoc and terror on the little town of Marnard—the shattered trees, the matted grass, the black slime...

"This is immoral," Mark's mother said.
And still the article continued:

> But what are these creatures? Where do they come from—these strange, shambling, humanlike monsters often ten feet tall and weighing nearly 300 pounds? Are they Neanderthals who have lurked in hiding for all these centuries? Are they the result of a terrible genetic accident?

> We don't know—but for the people of Marnard, the nightmare may have just begun. The creatures are loose, somewhere in the prairie along the rivers. And nobody knows where they may strike again—perhaps they already have. In nearby Rinkers Grove unearthly shrieks have been heard at night. Throughout the tiny community, blood runs cold as headless sheep appear in prairie grass...

Steve Scott set the newspaper down, his lips tight. Then he said to Mr. Velliers, "Any idea where this Kyla Raines is staying?"

"I believe she's at the Sylvan Arbor Motel. But what—"

Without waiting for him to finish, Mr. Scott took three steps off the porch in one leap. Mark ran after him, climbing into the pickup beside him. "You going to the motel, Dad?"

"Yes I am," Mr. Scott snapped. "I've a few words to say to a certain 'social worker.' "

The drive to the motel was short. Ms. Raines opened the door at the first knock. Her gaze dropped to the newspaper in the angry man's hand and she smiled a little. "I see you've been reading my work. I must apologize for my subterfuge. But a writer sometimes has to do whatever she can to get a story," she said.

"You call yourself a writer?" Mr. Scott shouted. "You've written a mess of lying trash. An article like this can jeopardize the lives and safety of those two poor kids!"

"Mr. Scott, calm down. I've done a lot of research and I happen to believe my story is accurate. Who's to say those creatures aren't some genetic throwback? If they are, people should be warned that they're out there."

"Come on, Ms. Raines. You don't really

believe that! I don't know how you can sleep at night," Mark's father cried.

"I sleep like a baby, Mr. Scott," Kyla Raines said quietly. "Good evening." She slammed the door.

4 "IT'S JUST A stupid tabloid," Tanya Bailey said to Mark. They were in Tanya's kitchen, having chicken salad for lunch. It was the day after the outrageous article had appeared. "Who believes what they say anyway? Like two-headed snakes found on the moon and stuff."

"Don't be too sure," Mark said. "Plenty of fools out there buy into this stuff. They're going to be peering into the woods and wondering if beast men aren't looking back at them."

Tanya laughed and nibbled a potato chip. Mark had always liked Tanya, but they'd never hung out together until this summer. She was a pretty girl, with red hair and freckles. She kept insisting she needed to lose a few pounds, but Mark didn't think so.

"It surprises me that Kyla Raines is still around," Tanya remarked. "I thought she'd sneak out of town after her dirty work."

"I just hope the Thomas boys are a long way from here," Mark said.

Tanya shook her head sadly. "That Edward was so sweet. He never bothered anybody. I felt sorry for him. I wish Ms. Raines had talked to me before she wrote her stupid story. I about freaked when I read about 'giant hairy monsters.' My brother Cody is hairier than Ed is. You talk about a guy looking like a caveman!" Cody Bailey was a champion weight lifter. He'd won the high school state championship in the shotput the year before.

Later, as Mark headed home in his pickup, he slowed behind Chuck Jones, one of Sheriff Poulsen's deputies in addition to Mr. Scott. Mark didn't have much respect for Deputy Jones. The deputy tended to go off half-cocked sometimes, like in the spring when he lost control of the posse. Now the deputy motioned for Mark to pull alongside.

"There's been a sighting!" Deputy Jones said breathlessly.

"A sighting?" Mark repeated. "A sighting of *what?*"

"Those critters, Mark." Deputy Jones frowned and scratched his bald head worriedly. "Out at the Kendall place. Jody was feeding her filly and there the thing was, out at the windbreak. She swore it was one of those Yeti things."

"Come on, Deputy Jones," Mark said. "Jody Kendall is always imagining things. At school, when a teacher is two minutes late she thinks all the teachers fell into the sump hole behind the faculty lounge!"

Deputy Jones looked uncertain. "Well, I'm just repeating what I heard..."

"I think I'd better run out to the Kendall farm and calm Jody down," Mark decided.

"Well, good luck, Mark." The deputy waved and continued up the road.

Mr. and Mrs. Kendall and Jody were at the corrals when Mark pulled in. As he got out of the truck, he announced, "Deputy Jones told me about your call. I just dropped by to see what's going on out here."

"Out by the meadow," Jody said, pointing. "I was feeding Princess a flake of alfalfa. I looked towards the windbreak and I saw this ugly, hairy thing hiding behind the trees and looking at me. Oh, my skin just crawled. I was so scared, I couldn't even scream!"

"Look, Jody," Mark said, "you went to school with Edward Thomas. He was just a guy, right? Surely you don't believe that dumb story in the paper—"

"I never liked him," Jody interrupted. "He was funny, you know what I mean? Not like us. He always scared me. He did, Mark. He *shambled*, just like the article said they do..."

"Jody, there aren't any hairy Yetis or anything out there in the woods," Mark insisted. "You probably saw a big dog. That lady wrote that fake story just to make money. She wants to paint this town as a bunch of dumb jerks."

Jody didn't seem convinced. Neither did her parents.

"Tell you what," Mark suggested. "I'll go check by the windbreak to make sure there's nothing out there."

Mr. Kendall looked worried. "You sure you'll be safe? I can lend you my rifle."

"That's okay," Mark said. He turned and quickly tramped through the field. In less than five minutes he'd reached the windbreak and the river beyond it. As he strode along, he noticed the broken branches and matted grass. Mark was sure they'd been caused by the fierce spring storms—not some monster.

Mark gazed around the empty, lonely land. He couldn't see anything strange. In fact, the scene was rather peaceful. Evening was near, and an owl hooted in the distance.

Then, just as Mark turned to go back to the Kendall farm, an unearthly shriek broke the silence.

Mark's face turned grim. "Hey," he shouted, "whatever joker is out there yelling, knock it off! You're just scaring people, and you could get yourself shot!"

Mark was answered by another shriek. "Bryant? Dunne?" he called. "What do you guys think you'll accomplish? I know it's a boring summer. But there's got to be something better to do than polish your Lon Chaney imitation."

Mark hoped the taunt would get a rise out of the trickster. But nothing further broke the silence.

Mark waited another five minutes and then headed back.

The Kendalls were waiting when he returned. In reply to their anxious questions, he said, "Some kids in the woods were shrieking like that ridiculous story said the creatures do. I think I know who the guys are. They're awesomely stupid."

Mr. Kendall put his arm around his daughter's trembling shoulders. "Well, I don't much care what it is that's out there upsetting my family. I intend to keep my rifle handy. Anybody who comes around here threatening us is going to end up with a bullet in him!"

"It's some joker in a rented monkey suit, I'll bet," Mark said.

"Then that's his tough luck," Mr. Kendall snapped. "My Jody was awful sick this spring. We almost lost her when that virus hit. I'm not having her and my wife harassed. Whether it turns out to be this Bigfoot thing or some local troublemakers, it's all the same to me. I won't stand for it."

Mark sighed, knowing that in Mr. Kendall's present mood, he wasn't going to listen to reason. Mark headed home soon after.

"Mom, Dad," he said when he got in the house, "we ought to ask Sheriff Poulsen to call a town meeting. He needs to get everybody together and explain that the story in the paper is a hoax. I was just out at the Kendalls', and Mr. Kendall is really trigger-happy. He's out to shoot anything that moves in the woods."

Mrs. Scott sighed. "Mark's right, Steve," she said. "People at the store today had that same attitude." Mark's mother worked at the Marnard grocery store.

"Then I'd better call the sheriff," Mr. Scott decided. "Sounds like this could get out of hand just like the alien scare did."

***

A lot of people turned out for the town meeting, which had been set for Wednesday evening. It had rained earlier in the day. But now the night was cool and lovely with wispy clouds floating in the night sky and even a few stars twinkling.

Mark sat in the front row with his father. Mrs. Scott was working late that evening.

Mark looked around. It seemed like most of the town was there. The Bryants, the Kendalls, the Velliers, Mr. Marston, the school principal, and most of the school-teachers were scattered about the room.

"Folks," Sheriff Poulsen began, "the reason we called you all together was to stop that crazy tabloid story from causing a real tragedy. The folks who printed that story must think we're a bunch of rubes. Well, they'd laugh even harder if they could see that their fool lies are getting us all to jump at shadows."

Tanya Bailey's mother, the town druggist, said, "I can't imagine anyone would take that story seriously. It's just a ridiculous joke."

Sam Velliers spoke up quickly. "You wouldn't say that if you had a grandson almost strangled by one of those critters. *Whatever* they are."

"Now, Sam," Sheriff Poulsen said, "we've been through all that. Jules Thomas was hungry, and he wanted a chicken dinner. He didn't mean to harm Hugh, and he didn't really hurt the boy. And you know it."

"I guess I should know what happened," Hugh broke in. "He almost broke my neck. I'm not too sure that tabloid didn't get it right. Maybe the Thomas boys aren't Yetis, but they're sure wild and dangerous."

"Hugh's right," chimed in Larry Dunne's father. "We almost lost a son to that brute."

Mr. and Mrs. Bryant agreed loudly.

Mark looked at his father in despair. The meeting wasn't going the way they'd hoped.

Henry Baldwin, the insurance man who used to be Steve Scott's boss, stood up. He'd always seemed like a reasonable man. But when Mark's dad had the nervous breakdown, Mr. Baldwin had fired him on the spot. Ever since then, Mark considered him an ignorant and backward person.

"You know," Mr. Baldwin said, "when I was a boy, something happened in Marnard. There used to be hoboes hanging around the railroad tracks. One morning we found one of them torn to pieces."

There was a gasp throughout the room. All eyes turned intently on Mr. Baldwin. Mark eyed the man too, but he was following his own chain of thoughts. Mr. Baldwin must be about sixty, he figured. So he was describing something that happened around fifty years ago.

"Everybody in our house was pretty scared. My granddaddy said it had to be a big, wild animal that tore that poor hobo up. Whole town talked about it for weeks. It was a long time before us kids were allowed in the woods."

Mr. Baldwin paused for a moment and then nodded slowly. "So here's the point. I'm thinking maybe there's been a tribe of wild things—like those Yetis—hiding out around here for years. Comin' out every now and then to wreak havoc. Just like the newspaper said." Mr. Baldwin finished his tale and sat down.

"I remember what you're talking about, Henry," Sam Velliers put in eagerly. "I was a young man at the time. Folks said it was a big bear that done it. But we always wondered if it were somethin' else..."

"Bears weren't around much on the prairie then," an elderly woman put in.

"I saw a black bear once when I was a girl," another woman remarked.

Mr. Kendall had been taking it all in and now he stood. "I say we all stay armed. I don't know what we're up against, and neither does anybody else. But we've got to take care of our families against *whatever* threatens us!"

At this, almost everyone began to applaud. The small room rocked with thunder more ominous than any storm nature could brew.

5 MARK AND HIS father walked to the pickup truck after the meeting feeling defeated. Most of the people half believed the stories about the Thomas boys being dangerous. A few even believed they were nonhuman creatures.

"Maybe it'll just blow over after a few weeks," Mark said, climbing in the truck beside his father.

"I hope so, Mark. But to tell you the truth, I haven't much hope. Ignorance is like quicksand. It pulls you in. That's why I took so long to get help when I was depressed. I knew some people would lose their respect for me if they found out I needed psychiatric help. I was depressed, crying for no reason, and I knew something was terribly wrong with me. But I was too scared to ask for help."

"Yeah. Then Mom finally got you to see the doctor," Mark remembered.

"God bless her for doing that. Dr. Ashton got me back to feeling glad to see the new day every morning. But do you remember how people turned on me? They almost *wanted* to believe I was some raving lunatic. Mr. Baldwin fired me—said he couldn't risk having a 'mental case' handling his customers. He really said that—no matter that it's illegal to fire someone for that reason. I went from being a well-liked, respectable person to 'crazy Steve.'

"Even some of the relatives gave me a wide berth," Mr. Scott went on. "Like I'd suddenly leap into the air and start baying at the moon or something. That's how it is with the poor Thomas boys. They look different; they sound different. So people fear them and even hate them."

"Yeah," Mark said, "but Edward was such a nice guy. He was getting to be my friend in school."

"Did any other kids befriend him?" Mr. Scott asked.

"Well...not many," Mark admitted. "They'd giggle or whisper behind his back. And a lot of people were afraid of him too."

"I think I've told you, Mark, how proud I am that you tried to be Edward's friend," Mark's father said.

"I wouldn't have, Dad, except for what you guys—you and Mom—taught me," Mark said.

"Oh, boy," Mr. Scott said, grinning. "That's quite a Father's Day gift, Mark. And it's not even Father's Day!"

When the Scotts were almost home, another pickup came speeding from the opposite direction. Bill Bryant was driving. The back of the truck was packed with his friends Larry, Chuck, and Marty, all from the high school basketball team. Even after Bill was kicked off the team as captain, most of his friends stuck with him.

As the Bryant pickup approached the Scotts, it slowed. Bill leaned out the window and yelled, "We've got the proof! We've got the proof!" Then the truck picked up speed, leaving a trail of dust behind.

Mark and his father exchanged worried looks. Then Mr. Scott turned around and trailed the Bryant pickup into town. They followed it right to Kyla Raines' door at the Sylvan Arbor Motel. By the time Mark and his father got out of the truck, the four boys were already talking to Ms. Raines.

Ms. Raines turned to glance at the Scotts. Then she gestured to the four grinning boys in front of her. "You're just in time to hear the good news," she said. "Or, at least, it smells like good news to me. These guys look just like they just won the lottery."

"Better than that," Bill said. "We got a picture of one of them, Ms. Raines. One of those instant snapshots!"

Even from a distance, Mark saw Ms. Raines' eyes glowing with excitement. Yet she kept cool. "You did?" she asked in an even voice.

"Yep," Bill said. "And you can see every hair on that monster's body!"

Ms. Raines narrowed her eyes. "You guys wouldn't be kidding me, would you?" she asked.

"We all saw the thing, Ms. Raines. But we knew we had to get a photograph so everybody would believe us," Bill explained. "We waited real quiet in the woods behind the Kendall farm. Sure enough, it came lumbering along. I think it was after the horses."

He turned and looked to his friends for confirmation. Then he hurried on. "Anyway, we aimed the camera and shot. It just froze for a minute, and then it ran crashing through the woods. We were real worried that we didn't get the picture. But then we looked at it and, man! It's great, Ms. Raines!"

"May I see the picture, Bill?" Ms. Raines asked.

Bill hesitated. "Yeah, but...uh...we figure it's valuable. Any paper would pay for it, don't you think?"

Kyla Raines laughed. "Don't worry, guys. I'll make it worth your while if this is the real thing."

Mark sneaked closer to get a look at the photograph over Ms. Raines' shoulder. It showed a huge, furry creature near the windbreak. It wasn't an excellent photo. But it was good enough to be frightening. The creature was manlike and, although the body looked hairy, tattered clothing hung on the large frame. The remains of a red checkered jacket clung to the upper body. The face was blurred, yet Mark could see long tendrils of dark hair, matted and dirty.

Mark remembered that Edward Thomas had often worn a red checkered jacket. But other kids at school had seen the jacket too. Mark just knew the picture had to be fake.

"Mmm," Ms. Raines said, "this picture is clearer than the one they took in Eureka in 1967. *That* creature was more apelike and was covered with hair. This uh...creature seems more human—except for the unusual height and the hairy upper body."

A cold smile touched the young woman's face. "Why should I believe this isn't a clever hoax? One of you guys wearing an ape suit. Maybe a fright wig?"

"*This* is the guy who almost killed me and Larry," Bill said.

"So this is really Edward Thomas?" pressed Ms. Raines.

"It really is," insisted Bill.

"Liar!" Mark protested.

Bill wheeled around. "You got no business here, Scott. Besides, you know I'm telling the truth. Edward Thomas never would suit up for PE 'cause he was afraid we'd see his hairy body. But me and Larry saw him without his shirt when he tried to kill us in the apple orchard. *And this is him!*"

"Yeah," Larry put in. "It's him all right."

Ms. Raines stared at the picture again. "You boys will *swear* that this is Edward Thomas?"

"Yeah," Bill said. Larry nodded.

"Show that phony picture to anybody who knew Ed Thomas, and they'd laugh you out of town," Mark said.

"I'll call my editor and see what we can offer," Ms. Raines said, ignoring Mark.

"It better be worth all our trouble," Bill said.

"Oh, I can assure you, you'll be happy with the offer," Ms. Raines said. She disappeared inside the motel.

***

Later in the week, Sam Velliers came to see the Scotts. "It's darned unfair," he grumped. "My grandson was the one who broke the story. Now that Bryant boy and his friends get the lucky photograph and a fat check for it!"

"The photo is a hoax, Sam," Mark's father declared.

"I don't know if it is or not," Mr. Velliers said. "All I know is that she gave us peanuts for our story and for Hugh's picture. Word's out now that the Bryant boy is flaunting money all over town. Darned unfair. I told Hugh to load up the camera with color film and go looking in the woods himself. If they're out there, we oughta get some pictures too. I understand the lady will pay for all she can get."

"It's rotten business, Sam," Mr. Scott said bitterly. "I'd want no part in it."

Listening to Mr. Velliers, Mark decided that the only way to stop the madness was to find out who the Thomas boys really were. If he could dig up solid information on their background, then he could debunk the tabloid stories once and for all. How he'd love to see Kyla Raines' smirk wiped off her face when her entire story blew up around her curly head!

Mark decided to start at Marnard High. He'd see what their records showed on Edward Thomas. There was no problem getting into Marnard. Summer school was in session for the students who had to make up failed classes. One of those students was Jeannie Bryant. She almost collided with Mark as she left her math class. "What are *you* doing here?" she demanded.

"Just getting something from the office," Mark answered.

"Must be nice to come and go when you want. Me, I'm stuck here all summer," Jeannie pouted.

"Yeah, it must be pretty rough," Mark said. But he really didn't care all that much. Especially after she lied about poor Edward Thomas harassing her.

Jeannie bit her lip. "Pretty rough? Yeah, I guess that about sums up my life right now. I can't remember the last time anything good happened to me."

Now Mark *was* slightly sorry. He didn't like to see anybody hurting. "What's wrong, Jeannie?"

"My dad hates me 'cause I had to take summer school and couldn't be with him in New York. My mom hates me 'cause she and my stepfather wanted to go to France this summer and my classes spoiled it. And even you hate me, Mark!"

"I don't hate you," Mark said. "I don't hate anybody. Hating somebody is like taking poison. It eats you alive."

"Can't you forgive me, Mark?"

Mark studied Jeannie for a moment. He was shocked to see that her eyes had filled with tears. "Yeah," he replied. "Let's just put it behind us."

"So can we be friends again?" Jeannie asked. "I mean really tight like we used to be?"

Mark hesitated. He didn't want to crush Jeannie when she was feeling down. But he couldn't lead her on. Finally he said, "I don't think so, Jeannie. I don't want to get tight with anybody right now."

Jeannie's pretty face twisted with anger. "Then how come you're always hanging out with that pig of a Tanya Bailey?" she shot back.

"Cool it, Jeannie," Mark snapped.

"Cool it?" Jeannie exclaimed. "Sure, Mark. No problem. You always thought you were such hot stuff. But here's a news flash for you: You really leave me cold."

Mark shook his head. One minute Jeannie was trying to hook up with him. The next...

"You know, Jeannie," he said, "for a minute I sorta forgot why I didn't like you much. Thanks for refreshing my memory."

As Mark walked away something hit him right between the shoulder blades. He turned around and looked down. It was a small eraser.

"You freak!" Jeannie hissed. "You'd better stay out of the woods. 'Cause when folks start hunting those monsters down, they're just liable to mistake you for one!"

6 IN THE SCHOOL office, Mark asked Ms. Brent if she had any information on Edward Thomas. "I wish I knew something about Edward Thomas' background. Then maybe I can discover enough to stop those stupid Yeti stories," Mark said.

Ms. Brent nodded sympathetically. "Isn't it awful? The real tragedy of it is that the Thomas boy was doing better every day here. It's a shame he wasn't allowed to remain a student and reach his potential."

"Is there anything you could tell me about Edward?" asked Mark. "I mean, do you have any idea where he and his brother even came from?"

"Well, when all this trouble first started, we did some checking in Bricante Grove," said Ms. Brent. Mark knew Bricante Grove was a small town about a hundred miles away.

"Bricante Grove?" Mark repeated. "Why there?"

"Well, for as little as Edward Thomas spoke, he did mention Bricante Grove a couple of times. Unfortunately, we were able to find out nothing about him there."

"Hmm," Mark said. "Well, thanks anyway. Maybe I'll take a drive over to Bricante Grove. Who knows—I might get lucky and find out more."

Mark figured if he started right now, he'd get to Bricante Grove by noon. If he spent a couple hours there, he could easily be home by dinner time. When he called to tell his parents, his mother said, "Okay, Mark, but don't be late. We're having pork chops, applesauce, and rice. And cheesecake for dessert!"

Mark laughed. "Now you *know* I won't be late!" he said.

Mark drove east across the mostly flat prairie country towards Bricante Grove. Arriving there, he found the town was much like Marnard, except maybe a little older. Lots of grand old Victorian houses hid amidst tall, leafy trees. You didn't find houses like those in Marnard.

Mark hoped he'd meet somebody who remembered the Thomas boys growing up around here. Maybe that person could describe what misfortune had put the boys on their own like that. If he could bring such information to the *Marnard Tribune* it might put an end to all the tabloid garbage.

Mark slowed as downtown Bricante Grove came into view. When Mark was looking for information, the first place he usually visited was the library. He figured that wasn't a bad place to start here.

The librarian turned out to be an elderly man with a small, neat goatee. Mark explained what he was looking for, and the librarian checked through his files. "The city records, births, and deaths are kept right here because we don't have money for a fancy city hall," he said. The librarian searched for several minutes. But he could find no Thomases born during the last twenty years in Bricante Grove. "Fact is," he said, "I don't even know of a family in town with that last name."

"I see," Mark said, disappointed.

"I've lived here in town for all my eighty-one years," the librarian went on. "Everybody says that what's not in a book around here is likely in my head. So tell me something about these boys."

Mark told him everything and the

librarian nodded. "I heard about the trouble over in Marnard this spring. People getting sick, farmers seeing spaceships landing and such. Some folks in Bricante Grove were stirred up too. Didn't want to go to Marnard for fear of getting the 'Mars flu', as they called it."

Mark put the tabloids before the librarian, including the latest one featuring the photograph that was supposed to be of Edward Thomas. "If I could get some information about the Thomas boys, I could put a stop to all this craziness," Mark said.

The librarian nodded sympathetically. "Of course the boys might not be using their true names. Edward Thomas sounds like a name a boy might make up—two first names really," the librarian said. He suddenly looked startled. "There's an Edward Thomas Sloan here in town. But I can't imagine he'd have anything to do with these unfortunate boys. I've known him and his wife, Julia, for years."

"Julia?" Mark repeated the name. "Edward Thomas' brother is named Jules."

"That's an odd coincidence," the librarian

said. "Mr. Sloan owns a large feed and grain store in town. He's very prosperous. A gentleman in his forties, very respected. No children."

"Would it be possible for me to talk to him, do you think?" Mark asked. "I mean, maybe the boys I'm talking about had some connection with Mr. Sloan—like working for him or something."

The librarian hesitated. "Well, I guess it wouldn't hurt to talk to him. He and his wife live at the edge of town—large Victorian house painted blue and white. You can't miss it."

Mark knew he was grasping at straws as he headed down the street in his pickup. He figured this Mr. Sloan would think he was nuts contacting him on such a flimsy connection. However, it was the only straw Mark had.

Mark found the house with no trouble. A housekeeper invited him in. Presently a handsome, portly man appeared in the living room.

"What might I do for you, young man?" he asked graciously.

Mark nervously told his story about the

Thomas boys—how their appearance in Marnard had inspired a springtime of panic. He explained how once again the brothers were feared as some subhuman marauders. "I'm trying to find out who these brothers really are so all the crazy stories can be disproven," Mark said.

Mr. Sloan nodded. "Commendable effort on your part, young man. I wish I could help you. Unfortunately, all I know about the Thomas boys is what I've seen in the tabloid. I don't read them myself, but I've certainly heard others discussing the lurid stories about Marnard."

"I just thought Edward and Jules might have had some connection with you," Mark said.

"It's interesting that they have names similar to my wife's and mine. Perhaps they saw our names in the local paper. We're very active in the community. They may have been picking aliases out of the newspaper and randomly come across our names," Mr. Sloan said.

A lovely woman with dark hair and striking blue eyes appeared in the doorway. "Ed, who was at the door?" She glanced at

Mark. "Oh, excuse me. Who's our visitor?"

"Oh, just a young chap from Marnard, my dear," Mr. Sloan said. "Nothing to worry about."

"Mr. Sloan was just helping answer some questions. I've been trying to get some information on two brothers—the Thomas boys," Mark began to explain. But Mr. Sloan's eyebrows lifted and he quickly whispered, "She's quite ill." That silenced Mark.

The woman stared at Mark. Then she swooned and groped for a chair. Her husband rushed to her side and caught her before she went limp. "She's been ill," he said again to Mark. "You really must excuse us now."

"Yeah, okay, I'm sorry," Mark said. He thanked them and hurried to the door. Yet as he headed out the drive, Mark couldn't shake his suspicions. He could have sworn there was a flicker of recognition in the woman's eyes when he mentioned the Thomas boys. He couldn't help wondering if the shock of hearing those names made her faint.

It was getting late, and Mark figured

he'd better start for home. But first he drove around Bricante Grove, stopping at the town cemetery and checking out names. However, no granite tombstone bore the name Thomas. Mark reluctantly gave up the search.

On the outskirts of the town, a large old brick building caught his attention. It was perched like a brooding vulture on a small hill.

Mark turned down a side road for a closer look at the building. As he drew nearer, he noticed that the windows were gone and even some doors were missing. The place had obviously been abandoned for some time.

Mark studied the building's sagging face. The late afternoon sun lit the interior, giving the building the eerie look of a long-forgotten Halloween pumpkin. It certainly wasn't a friendly place. In fact, it was a little spooky.

Mark stopped at the nearest farmhouse. He asked the lady who came to the door what the building was.

"Oh *that*," she said with a grimace. "For a while it was a warehouse, but they went bankrupt. Before that it was a hotel, and that failed too. Nobody wanted to stay there. It's such a grim place. You see, it was an asylum in the beginning—"

"An asylum?" Mark repeated. "You mean for mental patients?"

"Yes." She shuddered. "Awful place. I guess the ghosts have never left. Poor wretches used to live in there...poor, abandoned wretches."

Mark felt a sudden dryness in his mouth. "Where did the people go—the patients?"

The woman shrugged. "Who knows? Thank heaven they aren't *there* anymore, that's all I can say."

Mark gazed back at the building once more. A chilling thought struck him. What if the Thomas boys had run from *that* place? What if they were mentally ill?

That news certainly wouldn't stop the wild rumors about the brothers. In fact, it would just raise another set of fears and dreads against them.

7 MARK WAS JUST outside of Springville when he spotted the old cabin where his father had hidden the Thomas boys a few months before. The cabin door was open and Mark saw someone moving around inside.

At once, Mark slammed on the brakes and jumped out, running towards the cabin. "Ed?" he shouted. Suddenly the shadowy figure darted from the cabin and raced into the woods. Mark gave chase. "Ed! It's me, your friend, Mark Scott!" he yelled.

Mark wasn't even sure the person he was chasing was Ed Thomas. But if it was, he had to talk to him. It seemed now as though only Ed and his brother had the answers that would clear up their cloudy past.

Sounds of breaking brush and cracked branches rang in the air as both boys plunged through the woods. Ahead, Mark heard the soft thunder of the narrow river that headed towards the Platte. The heavy spring rains had turned the peaceful river into a raging torrent.

"Ed!" Mark shouted, seeing a flash of

blue-black hair. "Stop! It's me, Mark, your friend!"

Edward reached the river and leaped to a large white rock in the middle that formed a kind of island. Then, in another leap, he disappeared.

Mark didn't hesitate. He tried to imitate Edward's strategy—leaping to the rock, then jumping to the other side. But Mark missed the island rock and instead plunged into the wild waters.

Mark was a good swimmer under ordinary circumstances, but not in a swiftly moving river. He panicked as he tried desperately to grasp onto something. A terrible thought flashed through his mind: He was going to drown!

Gathering all his breath, Mark shouted as loudly as he could: "Help!"

Then, just as Mark had given up hope, Edward appeared on the opposite shore. In his big hands he held a thick rope. Quickly he knotted it and threw it towards Mark.

Mark desperately tried to grasp the rope. But the chill water had numbed his hands. The rope slipped out of his grasp.

With lightning speed, Ed hauled the rope back in. Then he tied one end of the rope to a stout tree near the shore. Tying the other around his own waist, he jumped into the river. He swam towards Mark with astonishing strength. Grabbing Mark's arm, he pulled it around his own neck. "Hold on, fren," he told Mark.

With seemingly little effort, Edward pulled Mark to the shore. With the help of the rope, they were soon scrambling onto the muddy banks of the river.

"Man," Mark cried, "you saved my life, Ed!"

"Fren," Edward said with a faint smile.

"Ed, I want to help you," Mark said.

"Go, fren, go now quick," Edward urged. He pointed downriver. "Easy cross. Go, fren."

"Ed, my dad and my whole family want to help you and Jules," Mark said.

The turquoise eyes glowed with a fear so intense that Mark knew he couldn't quell it.

"Go, fren. Go quick," Edward pleaded.

Reluctantly Mark got up and said, "Okay, but thanks. You saved my life," he repeated and held out his hand.

Edward Thomas looked down at the offered hand with a bewildered look. He didn't seem to understand the gesture. "You want?" he asked.

Mark gently grasped Ed's hand and brought it up in a firm handshake. "Friends," Mark said, smiling.

Ed managed another quick little smile of his own. "Frens," he agreed. Then he turned and disappeared into the woods.

Mark headed downstream, coming to a place where the river narrowed even more. There, overhanging tree branches would make it easy to get to the other side.

As Mark glanced back upstream, a thought struck him. He recalled how Edward disappeared so quickly after his leap across the river. And just about at that spot, there was a small cave.

It was easy to forget the cave existed. When there was a siege of drought, the brush died back from the cave entrance. But in years of normal or even excessive rain like this, the entrance was totally obscured by thick brush.

In years like this, the cave would make

a perfect hiding place.

Mark crossed the river and jogged back to his pickup truck. He arrived home as his parents were putting dinner on the table. "Mark! You're soaked and muddy— what happened?" Mrs. Scott exclaimed.

"I'll tell you guys after I shower and change," Mark said. "Don't eat up all the pork chops!"

Mark returned to the table in ten minutes and told his story.

"That was a dangerous and foolish thing to do," Mark's mother scolded. "You could have drowned."

"Your mother is right," his father said. "There's hardly anything as dangerous as a rain-swollen creek. The currents are unbelievable."

"I know," Mark said. "I was just so anxious to talk to Ed. I hate thinking about him—and Jules—having to hide and scrounge in the woods. It's not right," he declared.

"I ran into your chemistry teacher, Ms. Armstrong, the other day," Mark's father said. "She was telling me how quickly Ed had been catching on to the material.

She'd thought he was a slow learner at first. But actually she feels he has a rather good mind."

"There must be something we can do for those boys," Mark's mother fretted.

"I have an idea," Mark said. "Let's just pack a basket for them from time to time. We can leave it in the cabin. Maybe they'll slowly get the message that we're trying to reach out."

"That's a cool idea," Grace said. "I'll bake some chocolate chip cookies for them."

"Maybe Mom should bake the cookies," Mark said. "The last time you baked 'em we had to feed them to the cat. And even she wouldn't eat them."

"I've learned since then, *bonehead!*" Grace said. "I forgot the sugar last time."

"I'll pack some canned goods and a can opener," Mark's mother said. "I'll bet those boys would enjoy some canned vegetables, beans, and meat."

"Even simple things like soap and matches would be good," Mr. Scott said.

The next morning Mark took a full basket out to the cabin. No one was there, so he left the basket inside and drove home.

On his way back, he passed the Kendall farm. He spotted Mr. Kendall and his sons on the front porch loading rifles.

Mark drove in and parked. He watched in alarm as the Kendalls marched off the porch like an army.

"Somethin' out there in the woods spooked the horses," Mr. Kendall explained to Mark. "One of those apes, I reckon."

"Yeah," said the older Kendall boy. "We gotta teach King Kong he can't hang out in our backyard."

The younger Kendall boy patted his rifle and grinned. "This is the baby to teach him too." The thrill of the hunt shone in the boy's eyes.

"I'm coming with you," Mark said.

"You're not armed, boy," Mr. Kendall said. "Never know what those things'll do. That newspaper article said they picked up folks in Nepal and squeezed them to death."

"The story said a lot of stupid things, but I don't recall that being one of them," Mark said. He felt depressed at how the nonsense in the article was being exaggerated still more with each hysterical telling.

Next thing you know, he thought, they'll be saying that all of Nepal had been wiped out by Yetis.

Mark led the way towards the woods. "I'll take my chances with whoever is out there. Just don't get trigger-happy and shoot me in the back!"

For about forty minutes, the group stalked through the woods. The tension in the group slowly changed to impatience and then boredom.

Just as Mark was hoping the Kendalls would give up their hunt, he heard an ear-shattering cry echoing through the woods. "Eeeeeeeeaaaaaaaaah!"

Mr. Kendall's eyes widened. "You hear *that?*" His hands tightened around his gun. Turning to Mark, he said, "It's not human, boy. You best stand aside and let armed men take charge."

Mark was confused himself at this point. Surely even Bill and Larry weren't stupid enough to risk getting shot by playing these games!

"Eeeeeeeahuhhhhhh," the bellow came again.

"Steady, boys," Mr. Kendall warned his

sons. The boys looked not just tense but frightened. Their thrilling expedition was now turning into a nightmare.

"Dad," the younger Kendall son gasped, "what if we can't shoot it? What if it keeps comin' at us?"

"We'll blast it to kingdom come," Mr. Kendall swore.

Mark was frightened himself, mostly by the mood of the Kendalls. He ran ahead and reached the edge of the woods where the prairie stretched out flat again. There he saw a young man with no shirt on, his muscles rippling in the sun. Fine, reddish hairs covered his chest and arms.

The youth held something in his hand. Suddenly he reached back and sent it flying across the prairie with an earsplitting cry.

Mark glanced back and saw the Kendalls crouching in the woods. Three rifles were lowered.

There was no time to reach the figure on the prairie. So Mark whirled and sprinted back to the Kendalls. Hunkered down in the bushes, gazing into the sun, there was no way they could see what they were really aiming at. Mark had to reach them before...

He was close enough now to hear the Kendalls' anxious voices.

"There it is!" Mr. Kendall cried with a mixture of fear and triumph. "There it is— look at that thing—look at the muscles!"

"Never saw anything so big," gasped the younger Kendall. With a look of grim determination, he stood up and took aim.

8 "DON'T SHOOT!" MARK screamed. Even as the rifle went off, he jerked the rifle upwards.

Cody Bailey turned sharply and stared at his four neighbors. "What's goin' on?" asked the most muscular boy in Marnard. "What'cha all doing firing guns?"

"Cody! What're you doing out here howling like a wild gorilla?" Mr. Kendall demanded. "You almost got yourself killed!"

"I'm practicing the shot put," Cody said. "I always holler when I throw. That's why I come way out on the prairie to practice. It drives my parents crazy."

"We thought you were a Yeti," the younger Kendall boy said sheepishly.

"A *what?*" Cody Bailey asked.

"Those ape people they told about in the tabloid," Mark said sadly. "That's what the Kendalls thought you were."

Cody Bailey grinned. "Nawww, you mean it? You mean you folks really *believed* that article? I didn't think anybody was takin' that stuff seriously." Cody began chuckling.

"Stop laughing, you young fool," Mr.

Kendall snapped. His sons looked down at the ground, deeply embarrassed. Mark guessed Mr. Kendall was embarrassed too. Not to mention frightened that he'd almost been responsible for shooting his neighbor's son.

"Don't come bellowing around my farm again, you hear?" Mr. Kendall went on. "You're scaring my family. That's fine if you want to throw that fool thing and screech like a mule while you're doing it. But next time, stick closer to home!"

"Okay, Mr. Kendall," Cody said. "Sorry."

Mark remained with Cody as the three Kendalls marched back to their farm. Cody wiped the sweat off his brow and said, "Doesn't that beat all, Mark? First time anyone's ever wanted to shoot me for being too hairy. You just never know anymore what's going to cause folks to turn on you." He laughed again.

"It's not funny, Cody," Mark said. "It's an example of what fear can do to people. You stir people up, and you just can't be sure what's going to happen. It's like tossing a match on a dry field in August." Mark sighed. "The Thomas boys are different, so they make good targets. It's a real shame that woman came and wrote those stories. A real shame, Cody."

Cody stopped smiling. "I admit I was sorta scared of Ed when he was at school, Mark. I remember wanting to talk to him one day. He was standing at the cola machine and he didn't have a clue how to get a cold drink out of that thing. I wanted to help him, but I figured maybe he had that virus. Truth was, I didn't want to get near him."

"Lots of kids were afraid of him," Mark said.

"Yeah. You were the only one who really helped him, Mark," Cody said. "Man, I admire you for that."

Mark shrugged. "I don't deserve any medals, man. I probably would've been like everybody else if it hadn't been for my dad. Kids in the bus would whisper about him behind my back. I learned how bad it feels when everybody is pointing at you, and you're the outsider. I was able to feel for Ed 'cause of that."

"I guess," Cody said. "Be kinda good if we could all feel a little prejudice against us—just a taste. Then maybe nobody would pick on anybody else."

* * *

The next day Mark took Tanya Bailey skating in Springville. She loved to ice skate. In the winter she glided over the frozen lakes like a champion. During the rest of the year she used the indoor rink at Springville.

Mark wasn't very good on skates. But at least when he skated with Tanya, he didn't fall down. What Mark enjoyed most was sitting on the sidelines watching Tanya fly gracefully over the ice. She never looked prettier than when she was skating. Mark loved the way her eyes sparkled when she dipped and spun on her skates.

"You're terrific," Mark told Tanya when she came to catch her breath. "You belong in the Olympics."

"Nah," Tanya laughed. "I'm not dedicated like Cody. I'm not willing to give hours and hours to getting perfect enough to compete. I always tell Cody that when I go to the Olympics, it'll be to cheer him on to the gold medal."

Suddenly Tanya's smile faded. "Mark, I'll never be able to thank you enough for saving Cody from getting shot. What if you hadn't been there? Mom and Dad feel like that too." She planted a soft, sweet kiss on Mark's cheek.

Mark was a little embarrassed. "I'm just glad I *was* there."

Mark planned to stop at the cabin on the way home to see if the basket he'd left was still there. He thought about sharing the secret with Tanya. He was growing to care for her, and he wanted to tell her everything. But there was a deep sense of caution in Mark's heart, planted there by his dad's painful experience.

The Scott family had decided to share the details of Mr. Scott's illness with all their relatives. That had been a mistake. Most of the relatives were great about it. But Aunt Beryl went all over town saying, "My poor nephew Steve has got mental problems. I can't figure out what's wrong with him. Madness has never run in the family. At least, not in *our* side of the family."

Mark was sorry that his willingness to

trust people had been damaged, but it was. He couldn't risk telling Tanya that the Thomas boys were hiding near the cabin. She might unwittingly share that information with someone who couldn't be trusted.

As the cabin came into view, Mark slowed the truck. "I want to stop here a minute. I think I saw a red fox."

"Sure," Tanya said.

Mark jumped from the pickup and peered in the cabin. The contents of the basket had been taken. Lying next to the basket was a note that simply said, "Thenk you." Mark grinned and jogged back to the truck. He'd come back and pick up the basket later when he was alone.

"No fox," he told Tanya.

As they drove into Marnard, Mark saw Jeannie and another girl coming out of Marnard High. The morning summer school classes were just getting out.

Mark braked as Jeannie strolled in front of him with her friends. She was going against the light, but she didn't care. She turned and came over to Tanya's window. "How do you like going out with Mark,

Tanya?" she asked.

Tanya shrugged and said, "Okay." Mark knew Tanya didn't like Jeannie very much.

"You're lucky he likes...um...your type," Jeannie remarked. "Some boys really do like girls like you." With that, Jeannie laughed and hurried away.

"Don't mind her," Mark said. "She's just mad that I'm not hanging out with her anymore."

"I guess I could lose a few pounds," Tanya said.

"You're beautiful the way you are," Mark insisted. "Jeannie just likes to hurt people." But Mark could tell that Jeannie had managed to ruin Tanya's day. She was silent the rest of the way home.

That evening Mark told his family about the empty basket in the cabin and the note.

"That's wonderful," Mark's mother said. "Now we need to decide what to put in the next basket."

As the Scotts were talking, a van pulled into the driveway. A bearded man jumped out. Grace went outside to see who it was.

"Is this where the helicopter jockey lives?" asked the bearded man.

"Yeah, my dad," Grace replied. By this time another man had alighted from the van.

Mr. Scott stepped out on the porch. "What can I do for you?" he asked the bearded man.

"We need a guy who can take us for a chopper ride around Marnard," he replied.

"Sheriff Poulsen lets me use the chopper for other than police work, if you're willing to pay for the cost of running it," Mr. Scott said.

"Great. We need to fly over the river and the woods. Take some video shots of the area," the man with the beard said.

"You real estate people or what?" Mr. Scott asked.

"We're from a TV show. We do reality-based documentaries," said the other man, who wore wire-rimmed glasses. He held out his hand to Mr. Scott. "I'm Brick Anson. We're checking out this story about the wild creatures."

"That's all a hoax," Mr. Scott said sourly.

"Is it? Or is it just that you folks aren't anxious to be in the limelight? Don't sweat it. Just help us get some good video, and we'll be outta here. You won't be involved at all," Brick Anson said.

"The lady who wrote the tabloid story made it all up," Mr. Scott said. "You'll be making fools of yourselves if you do a TV story on it."

"Yeah?" Brick Anson said. "You seem awful uptight, mister. You got a problem with reality-based television?"

Mark broke in. "You mean those programs that pretend to be hard news and are really just tabloid stuff? They're great—for a laugh."

"Am I getting the message that you people aren't going to help us?" the bearded man asked.

"Right," Mark's father said.

"Okay. We'll find another chopper jockey. No problem," Mr. Anson said, leading the way back to the van.

"Oh, man," Mark groaned, looking after them. "Can you picture what a circus we'll have around here when those guys put the story on TV? Bill and Larry recalling their death-defying struggle with Ed Thomas!"

"It'll start all over again," Mark's father said. He shook his head in despair.

9 "DAD," MARK SAID, "I think I might have found a lead about Edward and Jules in Bricante Grove. But I don't think I can get much further by myself. Could you come with me this time? Maybe the Sloans would tell us the truth if you came."

"Sure, Mark, I'll come," Mr. Scott said.

"I've got a strong feeling Mrs. Sloan knows something, Dad. If we could get at the truth about the Thomas boys, then maybe all this crazy stuff would stop," Mark said.

Early the next morning, with the sky still red from sunrise and a feeling of rain in the air, Mark and his dad started out for Bricante Grove. They didn't say much on the long ride, but Mark saw his father nervously drumming his fingers on the wheel. Mark wondered if the madness surrounding the Thomas boys revived his father's own painful memories.

When the blue and white Victorian house loomed, they parked in front. Mr. Scott sighed deeply. "I hate going in there, invading their privacy. But I guess we have to."

"Yeah, Dad. I just can't think of anywhere else to find the truth. I thought of just going to the cave where the guys are hiding out, but there's no telling how Jules would react. He's not like Edward. I'd be afraid I'd push him into doing something desperate."

Once again, the housekeeper answered the door. And once again, Mark was led to the living room. A few minutes later, Mr. Sloan entered the room, looking none too happy.

"I've told you I know nothing of these boys except what I read in the paper," he said in a weary voice.

"I'm sorry for bothering you again, but...uh...could we maybe talk to your wife, Mr. Sloan?" Mark asked.

"We wouldn't have come if it wasn't terribly important for the welfare of the boys," Mr. Scott added.

"I told you I couldn't help you!" Mr. Sloan said, more loudly this time. "Now please leave!"

Suddenly Mrs. Sloan appeared in the doorway, apparently drawn by her husband's outburst. She glanced at Mark and said, "You're the young man who was here before, aren't you?"

Mr. Sloan hurried to his wife's side. "Don't upset yourself, my dear. These people are leaving now."

Mrs. Sloan shook off her husband's comforting hand. "I want to talk to them. I *must* talk to them. Don't you understand, Edward? I've been thinking of nothing else since I read that story. I can't sleep. I can't eat."

"Julia, you'll just make yourself ill," Mr. Sloan said. He tugged at her, trying to lead her from the room.

Once more, this time more forcefully, she pushed her husband aside. Then she came fully into the room. "For sixteen years this has been eating away at me, festering in my heart. It's time to shine some light upon it." She sat down on a straight-backed chair across from the sofa where Mark and his father were seated. "She was my sister," she told them.

"Who was?" Mr. Scott asked softly.

"The mother of the boys. They're twins. One was bigger, so everyone thought he was older. But they're twins. They are the twin sons of my sister, Esther. My dear little sister, Esther." Mrs. Sloan swallowed and her eyes filled with tears.

"Julia, you mustn't talk about it—you'll make yourself ill," Mr. Sloan pleaded. "Listen to me, *please!*"

"I've listened to you too much, Edward. God help me, I've denied my own flesh and blood because I listened to you! If those poor boys were hunted down and killed by some crazy mob, I couldn't live with myself. The truth must come out." She gave her husband a withering look. "No matter how much the truth damages our social standing!"

Mr. Sloan looked angry. But he kept quiet.

Mrs. Sloan gazed right at Mark and his father and her voice grew stronger. "My sister, Esther, had a very low I. Q. When our parents died in a car crash, I was already married to Edward. There was no other family. I wanted to make a home for Esther with us. But Edward said she needed more care than we could give her. He insisted she be sent to an institution."

"That brick building on the hill," Mark

said. He had just *known* that awful place played a role in this tragedy.

"Yes. She was only thirteen when we sent her there, and she didn't want to go. She cried and pleaded with me as best she could—she wasn't able to speak well. It broke my heart..." Mrs. Sloan gave a long, shaky sigh before she continued. "Anyway, when she was sixteen she was attacked. No one ever found out the details. But the result was that Esther became pregnant.

"Nine months later, she gave birth to twin boys, and she named them after us—her only family. Edward Thomas after my husband and Jules after me. She never gave Jules a middle name—I don't know why. Esther was a sweet, simple girl. In spite of what little we did for her, she loved us. She thought we cared for her."

"Now, Julia, we did our best," Mr. Sloan interrupted. "We always sent her clothing and things."

Mrs. Sloan ignored her husband and continued the story. "The children were left with her in that awful place until they were eighteen months old. Then a decision had to be made. The county said that children couldn't be allowed to grow up there in an asylum. I wanted to adopt them. I was never able to have children and I wanted to adopt those little boys."

Mr. Sloan put his hand on his wife's shoulder. "Darling, it couldn't have worked. Not *those* boys. They seemed strange, like *her*. And only God knows what kind of a father they had." He shuddered.

Mrs. Sloan glared at her husband, and he removed his hand. "Esther was told that her babies would be taken away and put in a foster home. But if those fools thought they could wean my sister from her boys...Oh, she loved them so fiercely. She cried and moaned for days. She clung to those babies.

"And then one day she and the babies just vanished. Somehow she managed to escape from the hospital." Mrs. Sloan lowered her head. In a voice mixed with sorrow and anger, she said, "For years I felt so guilty, so awful. I'd wake up at night in our warm, comfortable house and wonder how they were surviving. *If* they were surviving..."

"It wasn't our fault," Mr. Sloan insisted. "Having them with us would have ruined our entire lives. We weren't equipped to handle boys like those."

Mrs. Sloan paid no attention to her husband. "We didn't hear anything for a long time," she said. "I comforted myself with the idea that someone—some kind soul— had taken them in, all three of them.

"Then, about eight years later, Esther was found dead. She was lying by the river when some hunters found her. They reported seeing two ragged little boys with her. But by the time the police came, the boys had vanished. We found out Esther died of heart failure. She always had a weak heart, poor thing.

"Anyway, the boys had learned to live in the wild with their mother, I suppose. Time went by, and I convinced myself they'd somehow found a place for themselves. I forced myself to forget about them—it was the only way I could deal with it.

"And then I picked up that horrible tabloid," she went on. "I knew right away who those boys were. And I knew then what life must have been like for them, living like wild animals, without education, without even hearing normal speech. Esther hardly spoke, and even then you couldn't understand much of what she said."

Mrs. Sloan stopped speaking at last and looked down at her folded hands in her lap. Mark glanced at his father. Neither knew quite what to say. Finally Mark leaned forward. "Mrs. Sloan, may we put this story in the *Marnard Tribune?*" he asked.

"No! Absolutely not!" Mr. Sloan cried before his wife could answer. "It would violate our privacy. It would make our friends think we were uncaring monsters not to have helped Esther and the boys. It might ruin our lives in this community!"

"And well it should!" Mrs. Sloan said sharply. "Edward, for sixteen years I've thought only of *you,* *your* feelings, *your* standing in the community! Well, not now. Now I'm putting the welfare of my nephews first!"

She turned to Mark. "Of course you may print the story. Excuse me for just a moment." She left the room briefly and returned with several old photographs. "Here are my sister's babies when they were six months old. Here they are with Esther. Please publish them if they help."

Mr. Sloan glared at the group, trying to keep his anger in check. Without a word, he turned and left the room.

Mr. Scott said to Mrs. Sloan, "We're grateful to you for telling us your story. I understand what a painful situation this must be."

Mark looked at the photographs Mrs. Sloan had given him. Esther appeared to be a sad-faced teenager about his own age. Her big, vacant eyes stared back at him. The two baby boys with their dark hair were beautiful. "Thank you, Mrs. Sloan," Mark said, looking up at the woman.

"No," she said firmly, "thank *you!*"

Mark and his father went directly to the *Marnard Tribune* when they got back in town. Amelia Cohen, the editor, listened intently to the story. "Well, all right!" she shouted, her brown eyes dancing. "We'll scoop that rotten tabloid and pull the rug right out from under the jerks doing the TV show."

When the *Tribune* came out the next day, the photograph of Esther and her sons was on the front page. "Twin boys survive nightmare childhood and media lynching," the headline read. Mark had never seen the newspaper disappear more quickly off the stands. Most people felt immediate sympathy for the Thomas boys, but a few still clung to their fears.

"I don't care what made 'em wild," Mr. Velliers said. "I don't want them around here."

"If their mother was crazy, then they're probably crazy too," Bill Bryant said.

Mark grew angry when he heard comments like these. But at least people were putting their guns away.

A few days later, Mark and his mother took another basket out to the cabin for the Thomas boys. Although, Mark thought, the name Thomas really belongs only to Edward. He wondered what their real last name was. Whatever it was, Mark figured the brothers would always be known as the Thomas boys.

Mark had added a copy of the *Marnard*

Tribune to the basket. He wasn't sure how much Edward could read. But hopefully he could decipher enough to tell that the tone of the article was sympathetic. Maybe then Edward and Jules would finally decide to reveal themselves. Mark hoped that, little by little, the brothers would work up the courage to give civilization another try.

Mark and his mother parked in front of the cabin. As Mark went to the back of the truck to get the picnic basket, he heard a familiar roar. In a minute, the black MG had pulled up behind them.

"Oh no!" Mark groaned. "Mom, it's her! Kyla Raines!"

"Hi, Mark, Mrs. Scott," Ms. Raines said as she got out of the car. "Well, well. What a nice day for a picnic," she said, gesturing towards the picnic basket. "But that's sure a lot of food for two people. Perhaps you're expecting company? Anyone I know—or would like to get to know?"

"No," Mark almost yelled. "This is a private party, Ms. Raines, and you're definitely not invited. In fact, I can't figure what's keeping you around Marnard, period. Everybody knows your story was a joke."

"Come on, Mark. Be a good sport," Ms. Raines said with a laugh. "It was a good story and it sold lots of papers. That's the name of the game. But it's yesterday's story. All those papers are now wrapping garbage. It's time for a new story—an even better one. Boys raised by wolves. Or wild boys—can they be tamed?" Ms. Raines stepped closer. "They're around here, aren't they? Admit it, Mark."

"Please, Ms. Raines," Mark's mother said. "Don't you think you've done enough harm?"

"Mrs. Scott," said Ms. Raines, "I'm in the news business. I make my living finding stories people want to read. I'm not trying to change the world, okay? If I have a hot story, then I'm hot. If I have another boring piece about an aging movie queen's latest diet, then I'm as cold as yesterday's hash browns."

A grim smile crossed her lips. "So I'm going to find those wolf boys whether you like it or not. I'm going to get those pictures I want. And by the time I'm through, there won't be a paper in the world that hasn't smacked those boys on its front page!"

10 "OKAY, YOU WIN," Mark said, thinking quickly. "If you promise not to harass them, I'll tell you where they are."

"I promise!" breathed Ms. Raines.

"Well," Mark said, "the Thomas boys are holed up in a big brick building in Bricante Grove."

"Is that right?" asked Ms. Raines, narrowing her eyes. "Then why are you here at the cabin?"

"We just came back for our basket," Mark lied. He nodded toward the wicker hamper, which Ms. Raines had already spotted. He hoped Ms. Raines wouldn't try to look inside it.

"See," Mark said, "Edward and Jules were here for a time. And we were supplying them with food. But they realized that a lot of people knew this is where they were hiding out. They don't trust anyone to come near them, so they moved. If you read the *Tribune* story, you know that they were born in that building in Bricante Grove. It's abandoned now, but they hang out there."

"There'll be a nice little check for you

if this pans out, Mark," Ms. Raines promised. She hurried to her car and roared away.

When the MG's exhaust smoke had disappeared Mark turned to his mother. "She'll find out I tricked her," he said. "Then she'll be back here with a dozen jerks smoking the guys out of the cave— probably with bloodhounds! It won't take them long to smoke Edward and Jules out of that cave. Man, I wish we'd never even shown this place to her."

Mark's mother nodded. "I just wish I knew what to do."

"I've got to reach them, Mom. *Now,*" Mark said grimly.

"Please be careful," his mother cautioned. Mark nodded and then quickly plunged into the woods. In a few minutes, he stood at the river's edge. As loud as he could, he shouted, "Ed! I gotta see you." He continued shouting until Edward appeared, crawling from the cave.

"Ed, lots of people are gonna come here looking for you," Mark shouted across the raging water. "It'll be bad. You and your brother have to come with us, okay?"

Edward Thomas stared at Mark, torn with indecision. He seemed to be thinking of the time when men with guns surrounded him and Jules. Mark and his father had saved them then. But obviously the terror of that memory hadn't faded for Edward.

After a moment, Edward disappeared inside the cave, apparently to talk to his brother. When he popped into sight again, Jules was with him. Both brothers looked scared and nervous.

"Yes!" Mark said to himself, smiling with relief. He pointed toward the pickup and shouted to Edward and Jules, "This way, quick!"

The twins easily jumped the river. They followed Mark to the pickup truck and crawled in the bed. Mark quickly covered them with a tarp and then turned to his mother.

Mrs. Scott smiled at her son. "Well, I guess you took care of that!"

Mark grinned. "Let's go home!" he said.

***

The first steps back into civilization weren't easy for Edward and Jules. Just entering the Scott house made them extremely nervous. For their part, Mr. Scott and Grace were surprised to see the brothers. But they immediately tried to make the twins feel welcome.

"Have one of my famous fudge-nut brownies," Grace offered. She held the plate out to Edward and Jules. The brothers frowned at the plate. Then each took a brownie.

Edward took a bite. "Mmm," he said, smiling. "Very good."

Jules also took a bite. He smiled a little but didn't say anything.

Mark quickly filled Mr. Scott and Grace in on what had happened. Then he said, "I've been thinking Ed and Jules could sleep in the basement. It's carpeted, and there are a couple of beds down there."

"Good idea," Mr. Scott agreed.

Mrs. Scott said, "Those two definitely need new clothes. I think I'll run out to a store in Springville where no one knows me. I'd rather not have to answer questions about why I'm buying extra-large clothing."

"Well, they can't hide out in the house

forever," Grace remarked. "Where do we go from here?"

"All this is happening so quickly, we haven't had a chance to think," said Mr. Scott. "Any suggestions?"

"I think we should invite them to stay with us for as long as they like," Mark's mother stated. "Not many other people in town will even come close to them. So it's either here or back in the woods."

Everyone agreed. Then Mark said, "Mom, do you think Edward and Jules would let you cut their hair? Then they'd look like everybody else once they got some decent clothes on. Maybe people will finally come to their senses and see there's nothing scary about them."

Edward and Jules had been listening to the conversation in silence. Now Ed spoke up. "You cut?" he said to Mrs. Scott. His hand went to his hair.

Mrs. Scott smiled. "I'll be happy to. But first things first. You two need a hot shower!"

***

A few days later, Ms. Raines returned to

the Scott farmhouse. "You must be very proud of yourself," she told Mark. "You outfoxed a very smart lady."

Mark stood on the porch with his hands on his hips. Edward and Jules—complete with haircuts and new clothes—sat on the porch steps. They stared at Ms. Raines, though she appeared not to notice them.

"I have to leave town, Mark," Ms. Raines said then. "I've been sent to England to report on the Royals. Much more interesting than hanging out here in Hicksville. But before I go—just between you and me—where *are* the Thomas guys?"

Mark smiled. "They've gone back to the wolf pack that raised them, Ms. Raines. Didn't you say they were wolf boys?"

Ms. Raines stared at Mark for a second. Then she burst out laughing. "Outfoxed—and outwritten! I swear, Mark, you've got the real stamp of a tabloid genius. Just have to loosen up a little on those sticky scruples of yours."

Ms. Raines studied Mark silently again. Then she smiled and shook her head. "Guess I won't bet the farm on that happening. Not even one of the old

Hicksville homesteads."

With a good-natured wave, Ms. Raines turned and climbed into her car. And for the last time, Ms. Raines roared out of Marnard.

Mark looked at Edward and Jules. They seemed relieved that the woman had gone. She was the first person they'd encountered since arriving at the Scott house. It was sort of a test run for when they would really re-enter society. However, they still weren't very trusting. Any other time visitors had appeared, the twins had disappeared into the basement.

Now Mark said, "OK, guys. Break's over. We've got some more studying to do."

Mark and Grace had been working with Edward and Jules for hours a day, teaching them to speak, read, and write. It was exhausting work, but they all enjoyed themselves. Especially Mark. He figured he just might like to teach high school some day.

Later in the day, Hugh came over. As usual, Edward and Jules fled to the basement.

"Where you been for the last couple of

days?" Hugh asked Mark. "I never see you around town anymore."

"Oh, doing some reading, sitting around the house," Mark answered. Well, he thought, that *is* the truth.

"How about swinging over to the mall with me?" Hugh suggested. "Maybe hit the arcade, see a movie."

"Some other time, man," Mark replied.

Hugh frowned in disgust. "What's the matter with you anyway? Isn't this summer boring enough without you sitting around all the time?"

Mark didn't answer. He wanted to tell Hugh about Edward and Jules. But he couldn't. Not yet. Mark was relieved when Hugh soon left.

After dinner, the Scotts talked about the upcoming Marnard country fair. The family planned to introduce the "new" Edward and Jules to the town during the fair's square dance. There was one problem. Were the twins ready to face the people who had once been so hostile to them?

"Well, it's like Grace said, they can't hide out here forever," said Mrs. Scott.

"But I don't want to chase them back to the woods again either."

"Maybe we should tell people about them first," suggested Grace.

"No," put in Mark. "The townspeople have only one image of Edward and Jules: that of violent, hairy monsters. Telling them otherwise won't change their minds. We have to *show* them."

So it was decided.

***

The fair was held towards the end of summer. By that time, the twins had made great strides in speaking and reading. They were still frightened at the thought of the square dance. But they also were determined to become a part of civilized society. The Scotts had finally convinced them that going to the fair and facing up to the townspeople was the best thing to do. Mark and Grace even taught them how to square dance.

On the evening of the square dance, the Scott family accompanied Edward and Jules to the fairgrounds. Tanya also accompanied them. Mark had confided in her about the twins some time before.

The dance was going at full steam when the group walked into the big barn. Fiddlers were fiddling, and dancers were swinging around out on the floor. No one took much notice of the Scott group's arrival.

Mark and Tanya immediately stepped among the dancers. Grace took Edward's hand and gently led the nervous boy to the middle of the floor. Jules stayed close to Mr. and Mrs. Scott's side, a fearful look never leaving his eyes.

Mark and Grace had taught Edward well. He danced around the floor like a pro, switching partners and twirling as if he did it every day. For several minutes, Edward swung easily around the floor. He was just starting to smile when suddenly someone let out a sharp cry. It was Jody Kendall.

She stared at Edward. "I know who you are!" she cried. "You're Edward Thomas!"

The fiddlers stopped fiddling, and people stopped dancing. The room fell quiet as everyone turned to stare at the black-haired boy with the turquoise eyes. Mouths fell open in shock.

At last, old Sam Velliers spoke. "I see it, but I don't believe it," he said. He turned to his grandson, Hugh. "*This* is the Thomas boy you were talking about? This is your Yeti?"

Hugh just shook his head, too flabbergasted and ashamed to answer.

Then Mr. Scott stepped on a chair so everyone could see him.

"I'd like to introduce—or I guess reintroduce—everyone to some friends of our family," Mr. Scott said. "There's been a lot of talk about these boys—and a lot of silly talk. I think you can finally see for yourselves that there's nothing that frightening or that different about Edward and Jules Thomas."

Mr. Scott surveyed the room and then continued. "You all know their real story from the paper. And you know they've had a hard life. I and my family are determined to help them. We're going to see that they get an education. And we're going to make sure that they get treated like human beings.

"Now that you've seen them for your-selves, I hope you'll join me in helping them and in becoming their friends. They could use some, you know."

Mr. Scott stared down at the group of people. Everyone was silent for a moment. Then a few people began to applaud. More people joined them. Soon the old barn was rocking with applause for Edward and Jules, the boys who had managed to survive so many hardships and hostility—yet who were willing to give society another chance.

People stepped up to Edward and Jules and clapped them on the back, welcoming them to town. The twins seemed very uncomfortable at first. But when they noticed all the friendly faces, even Jules began to smile shyly.

Mark stood back a little from the crowd, letting Edward and Jules enjoy their moment. He was glad that fate was looking up for the brothers. But most of all he was relieved—relieved that the town had at last come to its senses.

Edward met Mark's eyes and strode over to him. Edward held out his hand,

and Mark took it in a strong handshake.

Edward grinned. "Thanks, friend," he said.

PASSAGES novels
by Anne Schraff